Siblings

by Magnus Florin

Translated by Harry Watson

Vagabond Voices
Glasgow

First published in 1998 as Syskonen © Magnus Florin

First published in March 2021 by
Vagabond Voices Publishing Ltd.,
Glasgow,
Scotland.

Translation © Vagabond Voices 2021

ISBN 978-1-913212-30-8

The author's right to be identified as author of this book under the Copyright, Designs and Patents Act 1988 has been asserted.

Printed and bound in Poland

Cover design by Mark Mechan

Typeset by Park Productions

The cost of this translation was defrayed by a subsidy from the Swedish Arts Council, and is gratefully acknowledged

The publisher acknowledges subsidy towards this publication from Creative Scotland

ALBA | CHRUTHACHAIL

For further information on Vagabond Voices, see the website, www.vagabondvoices.co.uk

Changeling Seventeen

Siblings

I was little. I went inside the pharmacy. It was silent. Dark. I moved around carefully. The smell. The preparations. Everything in shades of brown. The fine powder.

I went into the dispensary. I saw the fittings with pigeon-holes, receptacles on stands and the writing-counter. I saw the weights and measures, the poison-book, the telephone-ledger and the prescriptions which, according to the law, had to be retained for two years.

I saw the sensitive scales by the makers Bunge, Metz and Sartorius. In the centre of the room stood the locked poison cabinet with the variously labelled containers. *Acidum carbolicum, Chloretum ammonicum, Brometum natricum.*

I went through the dispensary into the decoction- and wash-room.

Then further into the preparation-room, which my father called the materials- chamber, with all the glass containers for medicinal purposes.

On a placard was the regulation which I learned by heart: "In order to fulfil demand promptly, every pharmacy should possess two or three unused jars of strong white glass, approximately 1,000 cubic centimetres in volume with ground-glass stoppers together with the lidded cylindrical tinplate receptacles belonging to them and a suitable wooden drawer."

I went into the tincture-room with its liquid medicaments prepared from drugs pulverised in spirit. On the lowest shelf were kept the red wines in bottles whose mouths gave off a rather sickly odour, like rotten wood.

Then down to the cellar and its collections of mineral water, acids, chloroform and liniment.

Up again and into the drug-chamber, which my father called the "hay loft", although it was not in the loft. Some labels were pasted onto the empty shelves: *Folium menyanthis, Folium sennæ, Rhizoma graminis*.

I continued into the inner pestle-room with its mortars of iron and stone. Tools for the cutting and crushing of medicinal herbs. A grinding tub with blades. A chopping knife and board. A half-moon knife and a knife with a curved blade, a large quern for coarse pulverizing and incising and bruising. Seven kinds of sieve, numbers 2, 3 and 5 of tinplated iron wire of different thicknesses and mesh, number 10 of brass, numbers 20, 30 and 40 of silk.

I went further, into the laboratory with the drying cupboard, distillation apparatus, evaporation bowls, decoction vessels, infusion vessels, preparation vessels, strainers. Pipettes for measuring the volume of liquids.

In the analysis room, the last one, and once I'd screwed up my eyes and slowly accustomed them to the dim light, I found my siblings.

Some of them were sleeping, their heads resting on their hands. Some of them were playing quietly with spatulas and vessels.

They were Ingvar, Ragnhild, Sverker, Rolf, Sofia, Sven, Gunhild, Nils and Gertrud. All nine of my siblings.

I said to them, "Come on now. We're going home".

January. Snow crystals formed on the window-pane. I looked at them. They were all different. All of them had something missing. Spines, legs, arrows, I thought.

It was snowing and in the hall the floor was getting wet from snow-covered boots. My mother said to me, "You must make sure you and your little siblings brush the snow off before coming in."

My schoolfriends said, "Your siblings are so quiet."

I answered, "My siblings don't talk. But they show me. I understand what they mean and tell the grown-ups."

My schoolfriends, "You're a funny lot."

I said to my father, "School isn't much fun. Can't I leave school and start as an apprentice in the pharmacy instead?"

If my siblings went off, I followed them. If they disappeared, I went looking for them. Every day.

I went to bed late at night and rose early in the morning.

My father: "Your wanting to be an apprentice in the pharmacy must mean that you're thinking of choosing pharmacy as a career."

Before long evening came and my mother asked, "Where's your sister Gertrud?"

I put on my outdoor clothes and went out. I looked in lots of places and called her name. I searched in Krafts Square by the Historical Museum. I searched beside the Elementary School Teachers' Training College and St. Peter's Abbey. I found her in Market

Square, where she was looking at the stallholders as they packed up their carts.

I said to her, "Come home with me now. It'll soon be dark and mother's waiting."

My father was a dispensing chemist and owner of the Lion Pharmacy on Lilla Fiskaregatan in Lund. It was a large pharmacy which grew its own medicinal plants and also made a certain amount of its own pharmaceutical products.

My father on the weights used in trade: "A *centner* is a hundred pounds, a pound is a hundred *ort* and an *ort* is a hundred grains."

February. It was snowing and on the way to school and back I got snow in my eyes.

As a sideline to the pharmacy my father ran a paint, chemicals and drugs business and made everything himself.

My father said, "Being an apprentice in the pharmacy is an important and demanding occupation."

I slept no more than a few hours every night.

Inside the Lion Pharmacy I could smell the odours of crystallised copper acetate, lead acetate, acetic acid, tannic acid, aqua fortis, sugar acid, wool fat, tinder, clarified pork fat, albumen, aluminium oxide, beaver oil and liquid ammonia.

My father said, "Remember to congratulate your siblings on their name-days. These are important days for them and they are pleased when we observe them."

I played with my siblings. We called to each other without words. Fought. Threw a ball. Shrill cries of enjoyment.

My father said, "You can be an apprentice in the pharmacy in the evenings and on Sundays and holidays. But only on condition that you stay on at school and do your best there to keep up with the lessons. Is that clear?"

I answered in the affirmative. My father continued, "In addition you must do further study of the subjects Latin, mathematics and chemistry. Is that clear?"

I answered in the affirmative. My father concluded, "Then I shall speak to the relevant teachers."

My siblings sat on the floor making noises. I listened and made out the words. My mother and father appealed to me. I explained to them what my siblings were saying, "They're saying 'hungry'. They're saying 'wee-wee'."

My brother Ingvar disappeared. I went looking for him. I looked in Clemens Square, along Kiliansgatan and on St. Petri kyrkogata. I found him at Central Station. He was sitting on the platform looking at the train to Landskrona.

My mother told me, "The lion sign hung from two

iron chains outside the door. It was stolen while at the joiner's for repairs. That was several years before you were born."

I saw to it that my siblings had jerseys and caps, that they ate up their food and that they went to bed on time at night.

The Latin teacher said, "*Iam seges est, ubi Troia fuit*. What does that mean?"
    I translated, "Now there are fields where Troy stood."

I played cops and robbers with my siblings. They never grew tired.

March. There was a break-in at the Grand Hotel. A hotel thief with an *oustiti*. I asked my father, "What's an *oustiti*?"
    My father: "An *oustiti* is a special tool with which a key left in the lock on the inside of a door can be turned from the outside. In this way the door can be unlocked or locked from the outside without access to the key. Do you understand?"
    I answered that I understood. My father concluded, "Take a warning from the break-in at the Grand Hotel and never leave a key in the lock."

It was the 10th of April. Still rather cold in the mornings.
Me: "Congratulations on your name-day, Ingvar."

May. The chemistry teacher said, "Natural objects are made up of constituent parts, which themselves are made up of simpler constituent parts, so that everything that is whole and composite can be divided up."

June. I smelt the fragrances of scorpion oil, carrageen, butter soap, Japan talc, soapwort and vanilla.
　　I stood in the dispensary and smelt the fragrances blending with each other.

My brother Sverker disappeared and I looked for him along St. Annegatan, by the Cathedral School and on Main Square. I found him by the Blind Institute, where he was sitting looking at the blind children.

The fifteenth of July. Heat. Ragnhild's name-day.
　　I told him, ""Congratulations on your name-day, Ragnhild."

I sang to my siblings, "We come from Ria-ra, Ria-ra, Ria-ra, we come from Ria-ra, aski daski da, we look for one of the daughters, daughters, daughters, we look for one of the daughters, aski daski da."
　　I asked them, "Where have Ragnhild, Gertrud, Gunhild and Sofia got to?"

I paid close attention to what my brothers and sisters were up to.

My father said, "It is your job as apprentice at the Lion Pharmacy to serve at the night hatch without seeking my assistance. The pharmacist must only be woken for urgent dispensing of prescriptions that have been issued."

My sister Ragnhild went into a ditch full of water on her bike. She hurt herself and her head went under the water. I pulled her out and saw to it that she got dry clothes. I said to my siblings:
"Look what happened to Ragnhild. Make sure you don't go into the ditch on your bikes."

My father said, "It is the apprentice's job to see to the application of plasters and salves."

I played with my siblings and sang to them:
"Now let's make a proper chain and who's going to be chained in?"[1]
I explained to them, "Now you have to say your names."

I was awake while the rest of the family slept. I thought that if I slept my siblings would wake up and disappear.

I liked studying the leeches, which were stored in the pharmacy's cellar.

I drew faces in ink on my finger-tips and showed my siblings, "This is you. Look how you're bowing and nodding!"

The mathematics teacher told us how Archimedes, when very young, drew small squares in the sand. I liked listening to his stories about the young Archimedes.

---

1 A game for children in Sweden.

It was the 27th August. Rolf's name-day. My mother shouted, "Lunch is ready. Where's your brother Rolf?"

I looked for him in Tegnér Square, along Stora Gråbrödersgatan and by the Bishop's house. I found him at Central Station where he was sitting watching the trains to Trelleborg.

I told him, ""Congratulations on your name-day, Rolf."

My father showed me the pharmacy's tools: "Here are the ointment scoops. Here are the scrapers. Here are the scoops for pills. Now show me how they are used."

I sang to my siblings, "We're looking for one of the sons, sons, sons, sons. We're looking for one of the sons, *aski daski da.*"

I asked, "Where are Rolf, Sverker, Ingvar, Nils and Sven?"

My mother said, "When the kite screeches there will be rain."

September. I could smell beaver oil, carbolic lime, fallen plaster, chalk, powdered bleach, carrageen and cassia fistula.

My sister Gunhild disappeared. I found her at the Institute for the Feeble-Minded, where she was watching people being admitted.

The chemistry teacher talked about sediment, filtration, washing, drying, heating and weighing.

My mother said, "Just think if you could manage to get your little siblings to talk one day."

October. My father explained the medicinal weights, "A pound is twelve ounces. An ounce is eight drachms. A drachm is three scruples."

My mother shouted, "Where's your brother Rolf?"
 I looked for him by the Cathedral and the University Library. I found him by the Deaf and Dumb School, where he was watching the deaf children.

November. The Latin teacher said, *"Repetitio est mater studiorum.* What does that mean?"
 I translated, "Repetition is the mother of learning."

I played games with my siblings and shouted to them, "Whoever's last has to start from the very beginning again."

The Statute of Pharmaceutical Products was kept in a special place in the dispensary. My father read aloud to me from the thirteenth paragraph of the Statute: "A copy of this Statute must always be available to the public in every premises where pharmaceutical goods are sold."

December. My schoolfriends asked, "Why are you so often at home instead of at school?"
 Me: "Because my siblings are often ill or upset. I look after them then."
My schoolfriends: "You're a funny lot."

January. My father said, "Read this Statute carefully. I'll examine you later on the contents."

The mathematics teacher said, "What would life be without arithmetic? Just a tale of horror."

February. I played with my siblings and called to them, "Hello, hello, are there any pots to buy here?"
 I explained to them, ""Now you have to reply by calling out: 'Yes indeed, there are pots, which colour would you like?'"

March. Evening. A clear, starry sky. My mother showed me: "The bright star there is not a star, but the planet Venus. It's the evening star until the middle of April and after that the morning star until Christmas."
 Me: "What happens then?"
 "It starts all over again."

I read in the Statute of Pharmaceutical Products: "In terms of this Statute, pharmaceutical products are taken to mean substances and preparations which are only or chiefly used as medicines or in the preparation of medicines."

April. It was late in the evening and I was staying up. My siblings were sleeping in their beds. My mother and father had also gone to bed, but my mother came up and saw me sitting there. She said, "You must go to bed now. You look tired and it's late. We'll all have to get up early tomorrow."
 I replied, "I'll go to bed soon."

The 15th of May. Sofia's name-day. Sofia disappeared and I searched for her along Stora Södergatan, by the Zoological Institution, along Bredgatan, by the Physiological Institution and along Helgonavägen. I found her in the park by the Isolation Hospital, where she was watching the people who were being cared for there.
  Me: "Congratulations on your name-day, Sofia."

When for the moment I had no tasks as an apprentice, I liked to look at the strange pictures hanging on the walls of the dispensary.

My siblings gradually began to talk. The occasional word. They only spoke to me. They did not want to talk to anyone else.

My father examined me on the Statute of Pharmaceutical Products. I quoted part of the second paragraph to him, "If usage of a product is found to entail danger to health, the National Board of Health may on receipt of a report either prohibit the import and sale of such a product or enact that it be regarded as a licensed pharmaceutical product."
  My father said, "I am pleased by the progress you have made in the pharmacist's field and by your diligence."

June. July. August. My siblings slept in their beds. I tucked them in and saw to it that they were warm and cosy.

Two other pharmacists in the city had been given licences. They owned the Hart and the Swan pharmacies respectively. My father never spoke about these pharmacists or their pharmacies.

The Latin teacher said, "*Ex nihilo nihil fit*. What does that mean?
I translated, "Nothing comes out of nothing."

September. October. I played with my siblings and sang, "Now let's make chain and who's going to be chained in?"
My siblings sang out their names loud and clear. Nils, Gertrud, Sofia, Gunhild, Sverker, Ragnhild, Ingvar, Sven and Rolf. All of them sang, "We shall be plaited into the chain."

November. My father was busy making his own cellulose lacquer. On a shelf stood the small bottles with the yellowish liquid. When you uncorked them you were first aware of the sudden smell of acetone and camphor, then a more gradual faint aroma of acid.

The 5th of December. It was Sven's name-day.
Me: "Congratulations on your name-day, Sven."

A cold winter night. My siblings woke and clambered out of their beds and said to me, "We're freezing and we can't sleep."
I saw how they were shivering in their nightdresses and said to them:
"You have to lie down near each other and huddle

up close together. Then you'll keep your body warmth better while you're sleeping."

My father was making Björkholm's malt extract in a special apparatus, fitted with tubing and a heating device, which was being fed with malt and water.

My siblings said more and more words to me.

I woke suddenly in the middle of the night and looked around the room. I got up and wandered around and saw how mother and father and all my siblings were sleeping soundly in their beds.

I asked my father, "What are those strange pictures on the walls in the dispensary?"
 My father replied, "They are Chinese numbers. Do you see? Can't you see?"
 I hesitated. My father went on, "You see now, don't you? Do you see? One. Two. Three. And all the way up to ten."

My siblings spoke more and more often to me. They also extended their talking to mother and father and also sometimes to certain relatives and to some of the regular customers in the pharmacy.

On the 30th of January. It was Gunhild's name-day. I said, "Congratulations on your name-day, Gunhild."

My father said, "What ingredients go into my cellulose lacquer?"

I said, "Your cellulose lacquer contains cellulose nitrate dissolved in acetone, together with camphor."

My father showed me how, with an ordinary playing-card, one could successfully scrape together powder residue on the counter of the dispensary. But he said that he was careful not to do this in the sight of the customers: "Such a way of doing things could give the impression that card-games take place in the pharmacy."

February. March. April. The mathematics teacher said, "Be careful at the start of a calculation, for if you make a slight mistake in the beginning it will gradually duplicate itself as the calculation continues and will lead in the end to serious absurdities which can only be cleared up by your counting everything again from the beginning."

In school my classmates said, "You have such little siblings."
I replied, "That's why I have to look after them."

My father: "The Lion pharmacy is a duty pharmacy."
He kept the night-hatch open all the year round.

I went looking for my siblings and found them in the corner of a backyard. They were standing there together looking at kites building a nest. The kites were swooping from high in the sky. They were bringing with them scraps of paper soiled with filth. They had found them, I thought, in the farmers' dunghills.

I could stay awake till dawn. On clear nights I enjoyed looking at the starry sky. How the whole thing revolved all of a piece.

My siblings sang to me, "Now we've plaited a proper ring and it will last our whole life long."

May. June. July. The mathematics teacher: "Only by rejecting the impossible does one attain the possible. You go from room to room, saying: it is not here, nor here. In the end you come to the final room and there you say: here it is."

My siblings said to me, "You are an apprentice in father's pharmacy and your path is staked out. But we feel lost. What are we supposed to do when we are as big as you?"

August. September. I received wages from my father. I bought fruit and sweets at Market Square and treated my siblings.

The eighth of October. Sticky leaves on the ground. It was Nils's name-day. I said, "Congratulations on your name-day, Nils."

I heard my father telling my mother indignantly that he had been passed a forged prescription.

My siblings: "You are going to have a proper job. You will earn your living at the pharmacist's trade. But how will we earn our living? We want proper jobs and trades too."

My mother asked me, "Where are your siblings?"

I looked for them and found them at Ribbingska Hospital. They were sitting in the grounds looking at the terminally ill patients.

The Latin teacher said, "*Si hi tacuerint, lapides clamabunt.* What does that mean?"

I translated, "If they are silent, the stones shall cry out."

It was the 4th of November. Rain and rough weather. It was Sverker's name-day. I said, "Congratulations on your name-day, Sverker."

After his training as a pharmacist, my father had taken over the running of the Lion Pharmacy from the late owner. His name was Möller. So my father was Möller's successor.

I smelt the odours of star anise, lignum vitae, oak-apples, gutta-percha, ginger and lard.

I showed my siblings their faces on my finger-tips. "Do you see when I clench my fists? I can hide you then, so you can't disappear."

A ton of Baracco liquorice arrived from Italy, carried by ferry and train. A thick liquorice extract was drawn off from it into three huge barrels in the yard. I could feel the pungent smell in my nostrils. I noticed my father's eagerness.

I said to my siblings, "This is a game in which the loser is punished. The loser has to speak backwards, or imitate five animals, or hop on one leg and call cock-a-doodle-doo."

My siblings: "We'd love to do all these fun things."

December. My mother said, "I want you to know that we are grateful to you for teaching your siblings to speak. They chat in a friendly way to the customers and yesterday I heard them talking at length for several minutes about how glad they were that winter has arrived with lots of snow on the slopes."

The National Board of Health made its annual inspection of my father's pharmacy. The inspector said to my father, "Three hundred leeches are in good condition. But the *Radix ratanhiae* is worm-eaten and the aromatic water *Aqua menthae* has lost its aroma."

After the inspector had gone my father said, "The inspector has eagle eyes."

January. I sang to my siblings, "No, look, it's snowing."

I did well in Latin, mathematics and chemistry.

I said to my siblings, "Remember that I am the eldest of all of us. I make the decisions on your behalf."

I quoted from the Regulations Governing Pharmaceutical Goods for my father, "A pharmaceutical product which has been furnished with a coating must be provided with a seal and kept under lock and key and in a secure place, until a legally binding decision is taken as to whether the coated article is to be regarded as forfeit."

My father, jokingly said, "May justice take its course, even if the world comes to an end in the process."

I heard my father telling my mother indignantly that the reason for an attempt to forge prescription had been his own cellulose lacquer, which had been used in such a way that a prescription handed in to the Lion Pharmacy could be used again after being dispensed, because the pharmacy's stamp could be removed imperceptibly from a surface covered with cellulose lacquer.

In school my classmates said, "You're always going about with your siblings."

I said, "I take care of them because they cling to me."

My father told amusing stories about the old pharmacist Möller.

My siblings, "Perhaps we'll be older than you one day. Then it'll be our turn."

I replied, "How could that be? The one who is oldest is always oldest."

It snowed and the snow lay on the ground.

The Lion pharmacy had a long history. But I knew that the Hart and Swan pharmacies had long histories too. I asked my father if the histories of the Hart and Swan pharmacies were as long as the Lion pharmacy's. My father replied, "The Lion pharmacy has the longest history in the city."

February. I was out in the snow with my siblings. It was by the Observatory. We were throwing snowballs and shouting to each other, "Yippee! Whoopee!"

We built snowmen. They had a carrot for a nose and pieces of coal for the eyes and mouth. My siblings were warmly dressed in coats and jackets, caps, mittens and scarves.

I said, "Watch you don't get your mittens all black from the coal."

They stood all around me and looked at me. I said, "You don't think that I'm the snowman, do you"?"

My father said, "During your time as an apprentice in my pharmacy you have live up to my expectations and I'm pleased that you've shown a consistent interest in the pharmacist's calling. I suggest that you now take up the study of pharmacology. As for myself, I can see that my career will soon be coming to an end. If you follow my advice you will have good prospects of succeeding me as proprietor of the Lion pharmacy on completing your education. What do you say?"

The 17th of March. Warm sun on my neck in the middle of the day. I said, "Congratulations on your name-day, Gertrud."

My siblings came up to me. There they stood: Sofia, Sven, Gunhild, Nils, Gertrud, Ingvar, Ragnhild, Sverker and Rolf. They said, "We've heard that you are to be a pharmacist and that you may take over father's pharmacy."

I replied, "That is correct."

My siblings said, "We're glad that you have found your path in life. But we're worried for ourselves. What are we supposed to become when we are as big as you?"

I studied to be a pharmacologist.

My father and my mother died. My siblings and I followed them to their last resting-place and grieved for them.

I took over the licence for the Lion pharmacy. I also took over the sideline in paint, drug and chemical production.

I employed my siblings as assistants. They were given hours of work, tasks to perform and appropriate wages. I gave them instruction in all the kinds of things they needed to know about.

I said to my siblings, "The days are passing."

I was glad that the old customers continued to visit the Lion pharmacy when I was in charge.

When I was teaching my siblings, I was careful to give them not only an instruction but also an incentive to act correctly.

Day after day I imparted my knowledge to my siblings.

I was pleased that new customers also found their way to my pharmacy.

I said to my siblings, "It may seem quite in order to weigh substances on bare scale-pans. But consider that strong-smelling substances and substances likely to cause staining will leave a trace behind them, so that when some other substance is weighed after them it will take on its smell or its colour from the substance that was previously weighed. The quality of the service will consequently be impaired. Make it your practice therefore to place a paper between the scales and the substance to be weighed."

My siblings listened attentively and made notes.

I showed my siblings the copy of the Statute of Pharmaceutical Products that was kept in the dispensary: "I want you to read these regulations carefully. Afterwards I will examine you on their contents."

I reminded my siblings, "The lips of the vessels and the stoppers must be kept clean. In particular jars of ointment with overlapping lids must be dried after each dispensing."

I allotted my siblings the task of serving at the night-hatch. I told them only to wake me for urgent dispensing of doctors' prescriptions. But I stayed awake and gave myself errands to the dispensary in order to check that they were discharging their tasks properly.

My brother Ingvar was inclined to spill things. In

weighing out the merchandise he was generous and also tended to spill it. He was good-humoured and light-hearted, and tended to take his time gathering up what he had spilt only to hastily and merrily serve the next customer. I watched this and told him that I had nothing against his good humour and that perhaps it couldn't be helped that things got spilt sometimes in the passing.

Ingvar said he was pleased by what he took to be praise.

I answered him in a sharp tone, "Under no circumstances can it be tolerated that spillage while serving one customer is left lying where it fell as you serve the next one! Everything that has been spilt must be immediately removed!"

My siblings quoted from the Statute of Pharmaceutical Products regarding medical drugs containing alcohol, "Medical drugs containing more than ten per cent of alcohol by weight may only be sold or otherwise given out from a pharmacy on receipt of a prescription from a qualified physician, veterinary surgeon or dentist."

I gathered my siblings and instructed them, "Bottles must be corked. It is not enough to affix the cork as a kind of lid; the cork must be forced a little way down into the neck of the bottle, so that the fumes from the preparation do not escape and the air does not penetrate the bottle."

My brother Nils said, "This is how to do it. Look at me, altogether."

With a sudden blow of his hand he knocked the cork

into the bottle. I turned to all my brothers and sisters, and said, "No. You should not, as Nils has done, knock in the cork, but rather press it down at the same time as turning it half a turn. If, like Nils, you knock the cork in, it can easily end up too far down in the neck of the bottle and be difficult to get out again. Do you hear, all of you?"

The Lion pharmacy continued, as the duty pharmacy, to stay open night and day throughout the year.

My sister Gertrud stood for a long time among the scales and weights. She asked me, "How do we know that the weights are correct?"
I replied, "There are standard weights."
Gertrud asked, "Then how do we know that the scales are correct?"
I replied, "They are checked against the correct weights. And if they agree with each other, that settles it."

My siblings quoted to me, "What is prescribed in the Statute of Pharmaceutical Products regarding medical drugs shall in relevant sections also be valid for ether and mixtures of ether and spirits, to the extent that such mixtures are not to be classified as medical drugs."
I said to them, "It's good that you are making a careful study of the Statute of Pharmaceutical Products. But I would encourage you not only to devote yourselves to the regulation concerning drugs with alcoholic content."

I noticed that a great many glass vessels were being used up and understood the reason when I happened to notice my brother Sverker handling a warm solution in a careless fashion. I gathered my siblings: "There are certain solutions that you must heat up so that the substances can be blended correctly with each other. But if you then pour the hot liquid into a glass vessel that has not been heated up first, the glass vessel in question can easily crack. It is important that you remember that cold and heat must never come together. You don't want everything to break, do you?"

My siblings said, "We would just like to quote one last time from the regulation governing alcoholic products."

I answered them, "Very well, then. But this is the last time."

They quoted, "Skin treatments with alcoholic content covered by the regulation concerning alcoholic preparations, and which contain glycerine, may not be sold with an alcoholic strength exceeding twenty percent by volume."

I said, "The dispensary. The customers."

I said to my siblings, "A good rule is always to wrap some paper round anything given out over the counter. It is not every time that the thing itself demands it. But it gives the customer a feeling that a transaction has taken place."

I said to my siblings, "You have become fixated on the regulation concerning medicines with alcoholic content. Have you any idea of the trade carried on in the inland parts of the country and in our northernmost counties with all kinds of medicines under the name of wormwood drops, Hoffmann's drops [3 parts alcohol to 1 part ether] and Riga balsam? Or Dr. Hall's drops, red mother's drops and Armagnac with salt? This disgusting trade? This loathsome business to the detriment and misfortune of so many unfortunates?"

My siblings: "No, we don't know much about those medicines. Tell us more."

It was my custom at night to rest on a mattress in the decoction and wash-room. In this way I could quickly be available for the urgent dispensing of prescriptions and could also see to it that the sale of non-prescription items was being carried out properly by my siblings.

My siblings said, "We understand that there must be a certain orderliness in a pharmacy. But must everything happen in the same way the whole time? There is so much that seems monotonous. We are falling asleep."

I replied, "If you can stand the repetitiousness for a while, then one day you will find that over time you have learnt a lot of new things."

One afternoon my siblings were not in the dispensary. I didn't know where they were. I looked for them and found them in the materials-chamber, where they were sitting close together. When I went in they looked at me. But they said nothing.

My brother Rolf was cleaning up with rags after a sale

of turpentine. Then he threw away the rags. I asked him where he had thrown them. He shouted, "I can't keep track of where I've thrown all the rags! Rags are there to be thrown away, aren't they? Do we have to keep tabs on what we've thrown away too?"

I replied, "It is of great importance to throw away rags in a proper manner, as they can easily combust after being used to wipe up varnishes and oils."

My brother Sven intervened on Rolf's behalf: "Can you tell us of a single instance where a rag caught fire without an exterior cause?"

I replied, "Most fires in pharmacies and businesses dealing in chemicals, drugs and paint' were caused by the carelessness or lack of understanding of shop assistants."

My siblings said, "We would like to read something to you from the Regulations Governing Pharmaceutical Goods."

I replied, "It wouldn't be something from the regulation concerning medicines with alcoholic content by any chance?"

My siblings said, "No, no. Not at all."

I replied, "Well. This will be interesting to hear."

My siblings quoted, "What in the first instance is prescribed regarding pharmaceutical goods shall also apply to trusses and other bandages, electrical belts and other such devices which have been designated as curative or palliative remedies for ailments."

My siblings asked me, "Now what do you have to say about that??"

In the course of serving a customer my sister Gunhild took a cork out with her teeth. I saw this and after the customer had gone I told her very sharply that this was not permitted. Gunhild replied that she had forgotten herself, that she didn't have the cork-extractor handy and anyway the customer hadn't noticed.

I reminded her that the rule applied not for the principle of the thing nor for the customer's sake, but for Gunhild's own health:

"You could become ill from substances absorbed into the cork and could even die."

Gunhild went pale and declared that she would never bite into a cork again.

My siblings liked talking for a while with the customers. I thought that in the process they sometimes became so loquacious that the service suffered, "It is unforgivable of you not to promptly finish serving someone when you can see that the next customer is waiting their turn."

I said to my siblings, "You were talking about trusses and electrical belts. You have also perhaps heard about Kurol-extract, Henriksson's health salts and Doctor Wilton's blood preparation? Or Kidd's capsules, the Volta cross and Alfred Eriksson's magnetic belt? Or Mattei's electromagnetic tooth-drops and Doctor Hartmann's lung remedy? Or Hans Bengtsson's remedy for rickets? Or the Auxilie-belt, Bertrand's Bull-powder and the Medico Vibrator?"

My siblings, "No, we haven't heard tell of such things. Tell us about them."

I said, "You should be glad that such things have not come to your ears. Clergymen have told me how, when they have been called in to dying people who have been ill for a long time, they have found the table covered in such proprietary medicines."

I said to my siblings that of course it was permissible for those who were serving at the night-hatch to rest occasionally and even sleep. But they should take care to rest and sleep in shifts, so that the customers don't have to wait to be served when they ring the night-bell.

The ceiling of the dispensary in the pharmacy was a good height and as the stock was so large and constantly increasing, I saw to it that all the available space was utilised. The goods were piled up in a heap with the help of cupboards and shelves which covered the walls and of cartons which were placed on top of each other. Nearest the bottom, up to barely a metre's height, were cupboards with many drawers that pulled out. After that came the shelves with their pigeonholes. The height from floor to ceiling was several metres and my siblings therefore used step-ladders and steps in order to reach the products that had been placed high up.

But sometimes all the steps and step-ladders were in use. My siblings then pulled out some pigeonholes and drawers and used them to improvise a step-ladder. The customers thought this was a comical custom and liked to laugh and comment on it. My siblings were amused themselves and believed that necessity knows no laws.

But on such occasions I was reduced to uncontrollable rage. Each time, after the customers had gone, I told my siblings that on no account were they to use the pigeonholes and drawers as a step-ladder.

My brother Sven said, "I like to have a bit of a chat with the customers. But with some of them you can never get a word in edgeways and it's insufferable to listen as they harp on endlessly about this and that."

I replied, "As an assistant you must always listen in a serious and concerned way to whatever the customers are telling you."

Sven said, "Some of them are never satisfied. It's a pain when they go on and on. You lose patience and instinctively want to bite their heads off."

I replied to him, "You must remain patient, even when serving them is stressful."

I found a playing-card on the counter in the dispensary and remonstrated with my siblings that, in the event that they had used a playing-card to scrape up spilt powder, they should see to it that the card in question was never left on the counter.

I said, "It would be understandable if such a thing was misunderstood by the customers."

My siblings asked me, "How does one get hold of guayacil drops, stomach drops and pimpinella drops?"

I wondered what could be the reason for their thirst for knowledge.

My siblings said, "Certain customers are really interested in these substances so we were curious to find out."

I answered them, "I suppose you know that your question refers to tinctures which contain alcohol?"

My siblings, "We know that."

I said, "Then do you also know that in this pharmacy we have extremely limited and closely monitored sales of such medicines?"

My sister Gunhild asked me if I didn't think that the scales and weights were really clean and shining. She said that at the end of every working day she washed and polished them carefully.

I told her not to use the corrosive polish, which could scratch the surface of the scale and make the iron in the weights rust. My sister Gunhild replied that our brother Nils sometimes used the weights as hammers and when weighing substances almost threw the weights down onto the sensitive scales.

I saw my brother Ingvar opening a bag by blowing into it. I gave him a severe telling-off.

Ingvar said that he never normally did that and just for once had forgotten himself.

I slept a whole night through, from eleven p.m. until seven in the morning. Woke full of unease. Went speedily to my siblings in the dispensary.

They said, "You hurt our feelings with your anxiety. Don't you believe we can take care of anything by ourselves?"

My sister Gertrud prided herself on being able to

decide within a gram how much a quantity of any product weighed. A lot of customers waited until she herself was free, as they liked to see her specifying the correct amount with such skill. The customers seemed to think that Gertrud was the best set of scales. All the scales in the country ought to be set by Gertrud, they thought.

But I did not approve of Gertrud's behaviour. I spoke to her of the gravity of the matter, "It may well be that many customers appreciate your talent for calculating the right amount. But the fact is that several of the older and more free-spending customers have made comments about you. Even if the weight you come up with always corresponds to the result on the scales, this does not mean that the scales can be put aside."

I raised my voice and spoke to all my siblings, "All measuring or weighing at random without a measure or scales is reprehensible. Apart from the fact that different quantities are undoubtedly being left out time and again, the custom smacks of slackness and therefore makes a poor impression on the customer."

Night. A clear sky, against which the moon, stars and planets shone strong and bright. I assembled my siblings by the pond in the Botanic Gardens. I said to them, "Uranus is in the constellation of Pisces. Jupiter can be found in the constellation of Aries. Saturn resides in the constellation of Sagittarius. Do you see?"

My siblings said, "Maybe".

I was angry that my siblings, when decanting from the larger storage vessels into the smaller receptacles on stands, were not taking sufficient care that the initials on the larger vessels corresponded with those on the smaller ones.

"How can I rely on you managing the next stage, and the next one is when you don't care about safety at the first stage?"

Night. I said, "Mars passes through the constellations of Cancer and Leo. You do see, don't you? Surely you do.'?"

My siblings said, "Maybe".

My siblings said to me, "Tell us about the ingredients in double wormwood drops."

I replied, "Double wormwood drops contain root ginger, St. Benedict's thistle, wormwood, dried Seville orange and alcohol."

My brothers and sisters, "How big an ingredient is the last one?"

I replied, "I knew you were going to ask me that. You should be concentrating on issuing prescriptions rather than asking questions about drugs containing alcohol."

My sister Ragnhild told me that she sometimes thought she could detect defects in the articles produced in the pharmacy. A powder didn't have the right graininess. A paint hadn't taken on the pigment. A solution was in the process of curdling.

Ragnhild said that in such cases she made a point of disposing of the product in the proper way or working on it to remedy the fault so that the customer got what the customer had ordered.

Ragnhild added that she always made a point of committing the defects in question to memory, "Then I am prepared the next time and I can avoid dispensing a faulty prescription."

I thanked Ragnhild for her attentiveness, which had undoubtedly prevented incorrect prescriptions that could have had unfortunate consequences. But I asked her not only to take care to commit the defects in question to memory, "You must also note down the defects each time in a special book. That book will come in useful later as an aide-memoire."

Ragnhild replied that everyone knew she had a particularly good memory: "I have never had a reason not to rely on my memory when it was a question of defects in the products."

I then replied that it was a mistake to always rely on one's memory. I addressed myself to all my brothers and sisters, "Don't be naive in that respect. For the memory can be defective too."

My siblings replied, "We will try to remember that."

Night. I said, "There is Jupiter with its moons."

My siblings said, "We wonder if you think we are all your planets."

I gathered that a customer had asked my siblings in a sarcastic tone about card-playing in the pharmacy. A playing-card had obviously been lying visible on the desk in the dispensary. I told my siblings in a sharp tone of voice that if in future they let a playing-card lie on the counter just once, I would immediately and for all time coming forbid this method of collecting spilt powder.

My siblings said, "How long have you been the pharmacist at the Lion Pharmacy? We think so much time has passed since all this first began."

My brother Sverker burned his fingers with nitric acid. He let out a yell and held up his blistered fingers. I instructed my siblings, "If anyone happens to burn themselves with corrosive acid the wound must immediately be treated with a solution of soda or weak ammonia and then thoroughly rinsed with water."

I said to my siblings, "You ought to be fastened to threads which I would hold safe and secure. Then I could reel you in when I wanted to. When it suited me."

My sister Gertrud got a splash of lye on her hands. She gave a yell and held up her blistered hands. I instructed my siblings, "For injuries caused by lye one immediately applies dilute acids and vinegar."

I went out on an errand. When I returned to the pharmacy none of my siblings were there. A notice said that the pharmacy was temporarily closed. Some time later my siblings came back and explained that they had only been out for a very short time.

My siblings asked me, "What is in *Collodium cantharidatum*?"
I replied, "The medicine you mention contains over ten percent alcohol by weight. And you are presumably not expecting more of an answer than that?"

I said to my siblings, "I understand that you sometimes

think that one day it will be your turn to take over the running of the pharmacy. That the Lion Pharmacy will one day come into your hands. That it will then be you who will be in charge of serving and dispensing."

My siblings said, "It's true that we sometimes think that. But sometimes we wonder if it must always be the case that something is taken over?"

The days passed.

I was out on an errand. When I came back I found the pharmacy in darkness. There was a notice saying that the pharmacy was temporarily closed. Inside the storeroom my siblings were lying asleep.

My siblings asked me, "What is in Wundram's toothache tincture?"
I replied, "Tea tree oil, peppermint oil, oil of rosemary, together with alcohol."
They asked, "How much of the latter substance is included?"

I asked my brother Ingvar where he had put the ointment spoons and the scrapers. Ingvar looked me in the eye and yawned.

I asked my sister Gertrud where on earth my brother Sverker was. She replied that she thought he had gone on an errand to Central Station.

I had problems gathering my siblings together. There was always someone missing.

My siblings asked me to come to them in the storeroom. Sven, Gunhild, Nils, Ingvar, Ragnhild, Sverker, Rolf, Sofia and Gertrud were there.

I said, "It is gratifying to see you all gathered together. That is not quite the norm nowadays."

My siblings stood silent. I asked, "What is it you want?"

Silence. I said, "Why are you not in the dispensary serving customers?"

My siblings said, "We have something to tell you."

"You are no doubt thinking of quoting from the ordinance regarding medicines with alcoholic content, long sections, forward and back?"

They answered, "No, this time it's something else."

I said, "Tell me then, if it is so important that you have to leave the customers waiting."

They said, "We have become tired of your pharmacy. We have no desire to be your assistants any longer. We want to do something else. You can stay on here among your chemist's goods and your oils. It's time for us to go out into the world on our own account."

I asked, "Where do you think you will go?"

"We are all going to pack our bags and go to Central Station and board trains there for Landskrona, Trelleborg and the rest of the country. Perhaps even abroad."

I asked, "And what are you going to do there? Do you think you will be better off just by heading away from here? Away to Spain, perhaps? Maybe to Holland? Or is it Bulgaria you're longing for? Or do you want to emigrate to Norway, possibly? What is there in Norway? Do you think you will be better off in Norway?"

My siblings responded, "Yes, You said it. We don't see why not."

I went into the pharmacy. Yet further in. Into the dispensary with the sensitive scales. The decoction and rinsing room. The storeroom with its glass vessels. The tincture room with the red wines. The cellar with the mineral water. The "hayloft" with the labels on the empty shelves. The grinding room with the mortars and sieves. The laboratory with the evaporation dishes. The analysis room, the last room.

None of my siblings were there. I thought they had already packed their bags. That they were perhaps already on their way to the Central Station. That perhaps they were already sitting on some train. That's what I thought.

Many days went by.

Months went by. I kept still and waited.

The 5th of December. Winter. Cold. It was Sven's name-day. But he didn't come when I called.

Sverker travelled north to Bjurholm and opened a paint and chemicals shop. He sold large amounts of spiced schnapps there to the local people. A person well known in the locality by the name of Hjalmar Holmlund bought several bottles of spiced schnapps from my brother and kept his intoxication going by means of further bottles of spiced schnapps.

Sverker also sold, for illicit use, methylated spirits,

eau de cologne, various mouthwashes, Riga balsam, armagnac with salt, cleaning fluid and alcohol diluted with oil of thyme and rosemary.

I made the long journey to Bjurholm and fetched my brother back to my pharmacy and to the waiting customers.

The 30th of January. Ice on the pond in the Botanic Gardens. It was Gunhild's name-day. I wanted to congratulate her, but I couldn't see her anywhere.

Gertrud travelled north to Eksjö and opened a business under the name of Eksjö Paint, Wallpaper and Chemicals Concern. There she sold packages of Henriksson's health salts. Each package of health salts contained three bags. The contents of the bags had to be emptied out together onto a large sheet of paper or into a mortar and then they were to be stirred together carefully and then sifted through a fine colander or a sieve.

Gertrud also sold large quantities of nerve-drops, Hoffmann's drops, red mother's drops, China drops and Doctor Hall's drops.

I travelled to Eksjö and fetched Gertrud back to my pharmacy and to the dispensary where the customers were waiting.

I said to the customers, "Gertrud will serve you."

The 17th of March. Spring was coming. The snow was melting. It was Gertrud's name-day. But she disappeared.

Ingvar travelled north to Malmberget and opened a druggist's which sold large quantities of medicines containing ether and alcohol. Queues formed in particular on pay-day as well as on Saturday and Sunday evenings.

I travelled all the way to Malmberget and fetched Ingvar back to the pharmacy.
 I said, "Ingvar! Ingvar!"

The 10th of April. Warmth. Ingvar's name-day. But Ingvar turned away.

Ragnhild travelled north to Jokkmokk and became an assistant in Jokkmokk's paint- and drug-store. There, she introduced the sale of the product Tussin, which borrowed its name from the Latin *tussus*, which means 'cough'.
 The product consisted of seven bags, containing in turn bird-cherry bark, coltsfoot leaves, camomile flowers, chervil, peppermint, yarrow flowers and polypody root, twenty-five grams in each bag. According to a printed instruction, the contents of the bags were to be emptied out and mixed in a bowl and boiled in three quarters of a litre of water for ten minutes. The liquid once cooled was to be strained and then drunk warm, diluted with five parts of water to one part of the liquid.
 The product was to be considered as a pharmaceutical product according to appendix II to the Statute of Pharmaceutical Products, under the group "Seasonings (teas) designated for blending", and might not therefore be legally sold in any shop other than a pharmacy.

Ragnhild also sold large quantities of "drops" to the locals, for whom they were a popular form of entertainment. Intoxicated individuals laid siege to the paint-and-drug-store. All around spread the stench of camphor, ether and alcohol.

I travelled the long stretch to Jokkmokk and fetched Ragnhild back to the pharmacy.

The 15th of May. The cuckoo called. Early morning shopping at Market Square. Sofia's name-day. I wanted to congratulate her.

Nils travelled north to Oslo and advertised Doctor J. Wilton's Blood-Strength-Preparation in all the Scandinavian daily newspapers. In the advertisement he wrote that he could show hundreds of testimonials from people who, thanks to this preparation, had been cured of all sorts of ailments. He based his business in Norway from where he sent pills to Denmark, Finland and Sweden. When problems cropped up with their export, he set up independent bases in Stockholm, Copenhagen and Helsinki. His preparation was a powder consisting of albumen, carbohydrate, phosphates, sodium bicarbonate, calcium and iron in the form of lactic acid salt.

I travelled to Oslo and fetched Nils back to my pharmacy. I said to him, "Oslo! Oslo!"

Warm days. The 15th of July. Quiet in the streets. All very peaceful. It was Ragnhild's name-day. I wanted to call her to me. But she averted her eyes.

Sven travelled north to Övertorneå and opened a shop there with Hoffmann's drops. The familiar smell of ether was spread over the area by drunken log-drivers and wayfarers.

I travelled the many miles to Övertorneå and fetched Sven back to my pharmacy.

Late summer. Cool in the forenoon and afternoon. The 27th of August. It was Rolf's name-day. But he made himself scarce.

Rolf travelled north to Köping and opened a grocer's shop where, in contravention of the Statute of Pharmaceutical Products, he sold the remedy Kurol-Extract with Lecithin.

Rolf also started up the cash-on-delivery sale of Thonérfelth's electric belts, Haig's medicine for inflammation of the throat, Kidd's capsules, Volta crosses, Alfred Eriksson's magnetic belt and Mattei's electromagnetic toothache tinctures.

I travelled to Köping and fetched Rolf back to the waiting customers in the pharmacy's dispensary. I said to the customers, "Here is Rolf".

September. When I walked along Klostergatan sticky leaves attached themselves to the soles of my shoes.

The 8th of October. It was Nils's name-day. But he failed to appear.

Sofia travelled north to Dorotea and took employment as an assistant in Widow Gustafsson's cafe. She sold spirits designed for mixing with soft drinks to the cafe's clientele. Upon interrogation it emerged that the spirits were usually consumed in Olof Nilsson's stable.

Sofia also took orders for Doctor Hartmann's lung remedy and Hans Bengtsson's remedy for rickets.

I travelled to Dorotea and led Sofia back to my pharmacy. I said to her, "I do not need to remind you of your tasks."

The 4th of November. Sverker's name-day. But he disappeared.

The 5th of December. Sven's name-day. No Sven.

Nights of frost.

Gunhild travelled north to Backe in Västernorrland and opened a store where she sold large quantities of Cyptol, which, mixed with fruit juice, was used as a means of intoxication and was openly sought after by the local people.

Gunhild also took orders for the Auxilie Belt, Bertrand's Bull Powder and the Medico Vibrator.

I travelled the many miles to Backe and fetched my sister Gunhild back to my pharmacy.

Gunhild, Nils, Gertrud, Ingvar, Ragnhild, Sverker, Rolf, Sofia and Sven were home. None of my siblings was absent. All my siblings were back in the pharmacy. All of their suitcases were standing unpacked and empty in the drug chamber for safekeeping.

Early morning. I assembled my siblings in the storeroom and said to them, "You have not been in Bjurholm, Eksjö, Malmberget, Jokkmokk, Oslo, Övertorneå, Köping, Dorotea or Backe. You have not been out of Lund. I have not been out of Lund. You have not taken any trains from Central Station. I have not taken any trains from Central Station. We have been here on the spot the whole time. Nor shall we ever go anywhere. The pharmacy is in full swing and you are still employed as my assistants. Now please be so good as to commence serving. The customers are waiting for you in the dispensary".

Early morning. The 30th of January. It was Gunhild's name-day. I said, "Congratulations, Gunhild."

My siblings remained inside the walls of the pharmacy. They served the customers. None of them made any more journeys.

It was early spring. The month of March. I stood watching my siblings. I observed them for a long time.
 I wanted to have them where I could see them. Inside my eye-sockets. Each single one of them. In through the cornea, in through the compartments with the aqueous humours, in through the iris, in through the centre of the pupil.
 In through the crystalline lens, in through the ciliary muscle and the conjunctiva, in through the white jelly of the vitreous body.
 In through the choroidea, in through the retina and its cones and rods, in through the optic nerve and into the brain.

So near should my siblings be. I wanted to see them every day.

I did not cease to keep track of my siblings' name-days.

I was gratified by the service to customers and by the production of medicines in the Lion Pharmacy.

I liked to let several hours of wakefulness during the night delay my going to bed and nevertheless to rise early next morning.

Things were as before in the Lion Pharmacy.

Spring came. Gertrud's name-day was on the 17th of March, Ingvar's on the 10th of April and Sofia's on the 15th of May. I congratulated them.

Summer and late summer. Ragnhild on the 15th of July, Rolf on the 27th of August. I congratulated them.

The pharmacy produced medicines and other retail products in the areas of paint, drugs and chemicals.

My siblings worked quietly. The days went by.

September. Zeal and industry reigned in the Lion pharmacy. I asked my siblings, "You are happy, aren't you? I'm happy. You're happy, aren't you?"

My siblings had pinned up a note by the entrance to the pharmacy with the message that they were out at the moment and would return in half an hour. When they returned I was sharp with them, telling them that on no account were they all to leave the pharmacy together.

They replied, "But it was only half an hour and we did write a note so the customers would know we would be coming back very soon."

I replied, "A duty pharmacy may not be closed even for a moment. In any case, how are the pharmacy's customers to know just when you're going to return, when you do not take the trouble to indicate in the note the time the message was written at? With such slackness, after all, half an hour can stretch out indefinitely into the future."

October arrived. I had no difficulty staying awake for several hours at night. But I experienced fatigue and listlessness. I wanted to watch my siblings go about their business and to rejoice in their work. Was not able to.

Nils on 8th October, Sverker on 4th November. I did not remember if I had congratulated them. When questioned directly they replied that, as usual, I had remembered to single them out. But their replies were so hasty that I had my doubts: "Is that right? Have I really congratulated you?"

Nils and Sverker: "Yes, you have congratulated us enough. Now stop asking us anymore. You are not our parents."

I asked my siblings, "You perhaps think that, at my

age, I should be busily devoting myself to all kinds of things?"

My siblings were needlessly slow in serving the customers of the pharmacy. They went on errands. They did not return at the agreed time. I dealt out reprimands and was met with silence.

I asked them, "Perhaps you think I ought to go to bed and sleep for evermore? And never wake up?"

December. Cold. I gathered my siblings in the storeroom. I said to them, "I have decided to give up pharmacy as a career."
 My siblings asked, "But what will you do instead?"
 I replied. "I can't be expected to know everything."

I stopped buying goods for the pharmacy from the wholesalers.

I introduced restricted opening-times.

I stopped making items for sale.

My siblings, "Shouldn't the night-hatch be open?"

I put up a note by the entrance to the pharmacy saying that in future the shop would be closed during the day and that sales would take place only by arrangement with the pharmacist.

My siblings asked, "Are the Hart Pharmacy and the

Swan Pharmacy to take over all our customers?"

I was unsure of my future life and career, and devoted myself to various hobbies. But I was not diverted by these hobbies. I thought they were dull and boring.

The days went by. I knew nothing.

My siblings said, "We have understood that you wish to close the pharmacy. But what have you envisaged us doing?"
 I replied, "I don't know."
 My siblings: "But we must have jobs. Shall we go off and try to find something for ourselves?"
 Me: "Wait a little."
 Them: "Forgive us for allowing ourselves to wonder."
 Me: "I don't know."
 Them: "If we go off you will just be coming to fetch us the whole time."
 Me: "You must wait a bit."

I saw to it that my siblings were within sight.

January. Heavy snowfall. I walked to the park by the Observatory. Children were playing with sledges, throwing snowballs and building snowmen. I spotted a couple of skiers passing. I waved to them and shouted: "Hey, have a trip!"

Many days went by.

On Södergatan I met one of the city's seven professors

of jurisprudence. As he was an old customer of both myself and my father, I spoke to him for a good while. He mentioned several legal cases that were occupying his thoughts just at that time.

I saw to it that my siblings stayed within reach.

I thought about the law.

I developed an interest in the outdoor life and joined the Society for the Promotion of Skiing and Outdoor Pursuits in Sweden. Its activities and aims interested me. I got myself a pair of long-distance skis with poles and made short trips. I encouraged my siblings to ski. I said to them:
"Perhaps we could take a little trip all together one of these days?"

I thought about the law as it was practised in our courts.

My siblings said, "We could perhaps get interested in skiing. But we can't follow you the whole time. We think we could go off on our own account. But wherever we want to go, you will constantly be hindering us."

I told my siblings how I was beginning to take an interest in the law:
"I intend to study to be a lawyer."
My siblings: "What about us, then? What shall we do?"

Me: "You can give up the pharmacist's profession. You can be my legal assistants. My little law servants."

February. March. All the rooms I went into. All the rooms where I looked for my siblings.

I listened out for them. In through the outer ear by way of the auditory meatus, past the ear-drum and the tympanic cavity, to the hammer and the anvil and the stirrup, to the oval window and the round window, to the tympanic duct and the vestibular duct, to the cochlea and to the fine threads of the auditory nerve and further into the hearing centre of the brain.

I went up all the steps to the entrance, where a doorman was standing watching everyone going in. With the old standard in his gloved hand. The ell which was the measure of all other ells. And past this doorman to the large central hall with doors leading in every direction.

I went into the meeting-room of the chamber of guardianship. Into the registry and the courtroom. Into the meeting-room of the magistrates' court. Into the chairman's seat. Into the rooms where the governor and the mayor spend their time. Into the tenancy committee-rooms. The administrative courts. Further in, into the supervisory sections.

I went into the archive depositories. Into the many small cellar-rooms adjacent to one another.

There, among the files arranged in rows by case-number, I found my siblings, furthest in, on the floor, huddled up near to each other. Some of them sleeping with their head resting in their hands. Some of them slowly leafing through case-studies, precedents and

verdicts from the different law-courts.
 I said: "Come now. Let's join up. We are going now. All of us. Together."

April. May. June. July. August. September. I was a law-clerk in the district court. I was a public prosecutor in the district court.

October. I gathered my siblings in the court and told them, "Between the law and a judgement that comprises an application of the law there exists the same relationship as that between the architect's drawing and the actual building of the house."

November. I wrote memoranda, law texts and commentaries on legal history.

December. Snowfall. I thought my siblings were not showing sufficient interest in legal and legal-historical matters. When I discussed questions of jurisprudence it might happen that my siblings would look out of the window and study the snow out there.

I said to my siblings, "The law relating to immaterial things is the same as patent law which is the same as protection of designs."
 They looked out of the window.

January. Cold. Snow. I asked my siblings about their interest in skiing. "Perhaps you would rather go on a skiing trip than sit in here in the court listening to me?"

Snowfall. I said to my siblings, "Study the 1899 law about protection for certain patterns and models."
They looked out of the window at the snow.

Snowfall. I asked my siblings, "Perhaps you would like to ski away from your jobs?"
They replied "We become sleepy sometimes when you tell us about the law. It is certainly true that we would rather go skiing. Won't you tell us about how you promoted skiing?"

I said to my siblings, "First comes the magistrate's court or district court. Next, the court of appeal. Lastly, the supreme court."
My siblings, "But what comes next?"
I replied, "Nothing comes next."

Substantial snowfall.
I said to my siblings: "Don't disappear from sight. If you disappear from sight, I will haul you in."

Persistent snowfall. I told my siblings about the joys of skiing. But also about its dangers: "Never go off on longer journeys without having sufficient proficiency and training. Allow plenty of time for the trip. Never ski alone. Stop travelling after darkness falls. ."

I said to my siblings, "A legal memorandum should be truthful, complete in its contents and in form short and intelligible."
My siblings replied, "Can't you give us an example? From real life?"

Persistent snowfall. My siblings said, "We would like to ski away."

My siblings: "But mercy exists too, so we have heard?"
Me: "That belongs largely to the realm of fantasy."

February. I told my siblings, "The lower court in the countryside consists of the district court, and in the towns the magistrate's court: the municipal court consisting of the mayor and councillors together with the administrative secretaries."

I said to my siblings, "It is not permissible in a memorandum to include dramatisations of this type: Deep in the woods, in an isolated house, lived an old couple ..."

My siblings: "We want to go off on a skiing trip. We like the heavy snowfall."
Me: "Take care. Don't lose your way. Watch out for the cold. Watch out for snow blindness."

I said to my siblings, "The upper courts are the Svea Court of Appeal, the Göta Court of Appeal and the Court of Appeal for Scania and Blekinge. The upper courts consist of a president and justices of appeal."

March. My siblings said, "Won't you tell us about the elderly couple, those poor, miserable old folk who lived so wretchedly alone in the forgotten house far away in the dreadful forest?"

I said to my siblings, "You must always follow legal

procedure and give an objective account of the circumstances. And never deviate from that."

My siblings asked, "Can you not give an illustrative example? Of how not to do it?"

April. I asked my siblings to think over this sentence:
"X must restore to Y a borrowed property with Z kronor."

May. I said to my siblings, "It is reprehensible, in the course of a statement, to attract the attention of a court with attractive parables of this sort: One fine summer's day two geese came waddling over Falsterbo market-place ..."

I remonstrated with them forcibly about this: "It is the facts of the case you should worry about."

June. I told my siblings, "The Supreme Court consists of twenty-four justices, three of whom are on the government's advisory council on legal matters."

It was the 15th of July. Sunny. Me: "Congratulations on your name-day, Ragnhild."

I lectured my siblings about performative utterances. And they said, "Give us some real-life examples."

I replied, "I hereby leave this clock to my cousin, so the clock will go to my cousin when I am dead. They appoint me a professor so I am a professor. I name this ship Queen Elizabeth, so the vessel's name is Queen Elizabeth. Here is money for fish at the market so the fish is mine. I hereby declare that I have taken over the country so I have taken over the country."

My siblings: "You say so many things at once. We can't keep up. Can we hear your story from the beginning again?"

My siblings asked me, "We would like to hear more about what happened at Falsterbo market-place. We would like to hear about the poor geese and the dreadful accident."

I lectured my siblings about dangerous and harmless things, "Is a flower-vase in itself a dangerous thing? When it is watered? When it falls from a window?"

My siblings said, "It's funny to think how someone can get a newly-watered flower-vase on their head."

My siblings: "You don't need to dedicate yourself to congratulating us on our name-days. We feel appreciated by you anyway."

Me: "You have always liked my compliments."

My siblings: "We liked your compliments a lot when we were younger."

I acquired colleagues in the law. We talked informally about all kinds of legal and legal-historical questions.

I lectured my siblings about conveyancing:

"Conveyance is the name given to the measure whereby a possessor conveys possession to another. Conveyance normally occurs with the knowledge and agreement of the receiver.

My siblings: "Give us an example."

Me: "One gives the recipient an object in his hand, allows his people to convey goods into his firm's stores, moves out of a house and gives him the opportunity to move in."

My siblings: "Tell us about when someone moved out of a house and someone was enabled to move in."

I said to my siblings, "It sometimes happens that conveyance is carried out without the recipient's knowledge.

My siblings: "Give us an example."

Me: "The recipient receives a letter deposited in his letter-box or plants planted in his garden, while he himself is away."

My siblings: "You don't have any plants. You don't get any letters. And you are never away."

My siblings: "Tell us all about that audacious theft of geese in broad daylight right in the middle of the square in Falsterbo. Tell us all about those cruelly and savagely and bloodily murdered old folk in that dreadful, dreadful forest."

I explained to my siblings, "The crucial thing is right of appeal. I lose in the magistrates' court. I proceed to the court of appeal. I lodge an appeal. I am given, or am not given, right of appeal."

My siblings said, "It's funny when you say that you yourself lose and lodge an appeal."

My siblings wondered if I could give them money: "A thousand-note? Just short-term?"

I asked them, "What is a pound?"

They replied, "A pound is money, of course, a note you can buy things with."

I told them, "The note is not the same as the pound. The note merely represents the pound. On the pound note you read that the Bank of England promises to pay the bearer the sum of a pound on demand. So the note is merely a picture of a pound.

My brother Sverker asked, "What happens if you ask the Bank of England to fulfil this promise?"

I replied, "Then you get another note with the same inscription and so on ad infinitum. You never get the actual pound."

March. I told my siblings about how daily life is full of legal proceedings: "For example, you lend an item to someone."

My siblings: "It's true that we are your siblings. But it's also the case that we are men and women in our own right. Those people who once were our schoolfriends have long since started a family and found jobs and professions for themselves. We want families and professions too. But we have nothing.

Me: "You are my assistants. You have your duties. You receive salaries for your trouble. And you have me to turn to. What more do you want?"

I took up with my siblings the question of casting lots in the administration of justice in the case of a large number of accused, as in trials following acts of war: "Many experienced lawyers advocate the casting of lots in such cases, as casting lots has the power to save the great majority among a crowd of equally guilty parties from the death penalty, while at the same time allowing all of them to experience the fear of death."

My siblings replied, "We become frightened when you talk like that. It's as if you are talking about us. Why do you talk like that about us?"

I lectured my siblings about so-called exemplary punishment, "A person who has committed murder by arson is sentenced to death by fire. Someone guilty of assault loses the hand which committed the assault. A forger is tied to the stake with the false coin in his hand. A woman who has committed an act of arson which has been discovered straight away is sentenced to stand at the scene of the fire for two hours a day for six days and nights with a lit fuse in her hand. Someone guilty of pilfering cabbages is sentenced to carry a cabbage in his hand. A couple of goose thieves have to stand by the door of the town-hall with a goose under each arm. A forger of banknotes is exhibited outside the bank. A kitchen boy has to husk rice in front of the kitchen.

My siblings: "We can't defend ourselves against everything you say."

Me: "It's the 10th of April. Ingvar's name-day. I'm inviting you all for some cake. Everyone must be there. Everyone must eat a lot of cake."

My siblings: "Is there anything that you think can't be seen as a legal proceeding?"

I gave my siblings an account of several different cases of injuries that occurred during work, "Injury caused by threshing-machines, a landslip while digging a canal, steel splinters thrown off by a machine, injury caused by a mincing-machine, a defective safety-rail on so-called French windows, a belt pulley that has come apart, a defective cable and winch spool, insufficient rope tackle, a falling so-called spindle-skein, falling down a lift-shaft and injury from a tile-making machine."

My siblings: "Have you seen all that? Who died? Were you there? What were they called? When did it happen? Where did they come from? Who survived?"

My siblings asked, "How does one become a judge?"

I replied, "A lawyer is appointed to a particular post as a judge and thereby becomes a judge."

My siblings asked, "How does a judge decide what is just?"

I replied, "The operation of justice is regarded as taking place because the law says that it shall take place."

I asked my siblings, "You will stay on here now, won't you, as my obedient little siblings?"

My siblings responded, "You, take care that we don't run off and become goose-thieves, arsonists and forgers."

I encouraged my siblings to think about the following questions: "Am I swimming because I have fallen in the water or so that I don't drown? Am I taking medicine because I am ill or in order to be healthy?"

My siblings replied, "We have never seen you swimming. We have never seen you ill."

My sister Sofia said that a few hundred kronor would do as a loan. I told her, "A Turkish piastre is divided into forty paras. The same holds true in Egypt, where a hundred piastres make one pound, but a Peruvian pound is divided into ten sols or a thousand centavos, and it takes a hundred paras to make one Serbian dinar."

My siblings: "We are your assistants. But you must tell us more about what we have to do. As things are, we so easily become drowsy and can't keep ourselves alert and ready."

I gave my siblings an account of certain lawsuits which I had committed to memory: "His engine has blown up and another person has thereby been injured. His horse has kicked another person. A container in his possession has leaked liquid. Smoke or gases have escaped from his factory, causing another person to suffer ill-effects. His soda-water siphon explodes and injures a guest. A rotten tree on his land is blown over and in falling injures a third party."

My siblings: "Sometimes when you talk about the law, we think you want us to carry out some errands for you. Or that you want us to sing for you and clap our hands."

Ragnhild complained of a headache and feeling faint. I advised her, "Don't postpone sorting out some insurance. You never know how long you'll be able to keep your health."

My brother Sven said that a fifty-note wouldn't come amiss. I told him, "In the United States of America a dollar is divided into a hundred cents."

My siblings: "Perhaps one is only an assistant to a lawyer for a certain limited period in the course of one's life? Perhaps one does something else afterwards?"

I said to my siblings, "Look at my finger-tips. There you sit, holding on tight. Look, how you're nearly falling off. Now you're falling off. Now I'm saving you. What luck that I saved you."

My sister Gunhild wondered if I could lend them a few kronor, just for a couple of days.

I brought up a number of legal cases with my siblings: "The licensee of a petrol-station responsible for damage to a car, arising from the fact that the petrol was not inserted into the car with the appropriate degree of care. The seller of a demijohn of hydrochloric acid sentenced to pay compensation as a consequence of carelessness in the delivery to the buyer, in that the hire-car driver in charge of the delivery dropped the demijohn on the stairs of the buyer's business premises, whereby the staircase was damaged. A hotelier responsible for sums of money handed over to a porter, and given by him to an embezzling messenger-boy."

My siblings: "We don't like it when you blame us. Not everything is our fault, is it?"

May. June. July. August. September. October. November. December. January. I said to my siblings, "Look, it's snowing."

I asked my siblings to listen to an imaginary legal case, "I order goods by phone and claim to be the representative of a certain firm. When the goods are collected, I sign the invoice with the name of the imaginary person with the intention of avoiding being responsible for fraud. The question now is, is this to be regarded as false attestation or forgery of a document?"

I asked my siblings, "According to Kant's teaching, the main purpose of punishment is a) retribution b) deterrence c) reform?"

My siblings asked, "Aren't you going to take yourself out on a skiing tour?"

The days went by.

My siblings: "We have passed the driving-test. We have practised driving in the driving-school's practice vehicles. But will we ever be allowed to drive around in our own cars? We want Mercedes-Benzes, Fords and Volvos. We want to drive where we like to wherever we choose."

Months.

I was constantly employed as a legal expert in a large number of cases within the field of immaterial property law.

Many years went by.

Winter. My siblings gathered in the law-court and asked me to come. Ingvar, Ragnhild, Sverker, Rolf, Sofia, Sven, Gunhild, Nils and Gertrud were there. I asked them jokingly, "Do you by any chance want me to say something about Falsterbo Square?"

They answered, "We are tired of being your assistants. We don't want to be here. We want to live our own lives. You can find yourself other legal assistants. We want to be somewhere else and you are not to come after us. Stay here with your law-books that you are so fond of."

I asked, "Are you leaving? But you belong here! Why do you want to leave? This is where you live!"

My siblings packed their bags. They said, "We are travelling away from you, one after the other. One by one we are going to go to Central Station to buy train tickets and travel away from you."

I imagined the different courts of law as a little series of places standing in a particular relationship to each other. I come to one place and if I don't like it there, I am referred on to the next place. And if I don't like it there, I am referred on to a third place. But from that place I cannot be referred any further. It is the last place and I have to like it there.

That was what I thought of the different courts of law.

I went in. Into the sensory organs connected by the fine sensory nerves. Into the lower courts and on into the upper courts. From the municipal court to the Court of Appeal. Then further on to the Supreme Court. To each and every one of the twenty-four judges of the Supreme Court. In through the epidermis and past the underlying derm. Further in through the connective tissue of the derm to the body inside. Into the brain and its thoughts.

November turning into December. Rain. The first to leave was my brother Ingvar. My other siblings wished him luck. He caught the train and they waved him goodbye at Central Station. He headed north.

The 5th of December. Sven's name-day. We skipped the congratulations.

Ingvar got a job unloading goods at the Customs post at Norra Hammarby harbour in Stockholm. Eight bales of carpets belonging to the trading company of Ringström & Kahn were unloaded from a ship at the quay.
  Ingvar's job was to take the eight bales of carpets to Customs for payment of duty. After the payment of duty only seven bales of carpets were recovered. The eighth bale of carpets was found in Ingvar's home.
  Ingvar maintained that the bale of carpets in his home was a quite different bale of carpets.

He was tried in the magistrates' court. I represented Ringström & Kahn and led the case against him.

The magistrates' court sentenced him. He was sent to prison.

I called my remaining eight siblings to me:
"See what happened to Ingvar?"

My siblings did not stop going to Central Station. My brother Sverker took the train north to Strängnäs. My siblings gave him a fine packed lunch as a leaving present.

The 30th of January. Snow. Gunhild's name-day. No congratulations.

Sverker took a job as a ferryman in the Strängnäs Sound between Tosterön and Strängnäs. One day a horse and cart were transported from the mainland to the island. There was a strong wind. After the ferry had set off it started swaying. A barrel of tar in the forward section of the ferry became unstable and fell with immense force against the horse's leg. The cart was then pushed backwards over the rail of the ferry, taking the horse with it as it fell. The horse died.

My brother Sverker was tried in the district court. I represented the horse's owner.

The district court rightly found my brother guilty. Sverker was sentenced to jail.

I called my remaining seven siblings to me: "See what happened to Sverker!"

They replied, "You don't want us to leave you. But it's not your decision. We'll go where we want."

My brother Rolf packed his bag and took the train north to Köping.

The 17th of March. Rain. Gertrud's name-day. No congratulations.

In Köping, Rolf found work as a driver. His job was to drive a lorry from one place to another. He let someone come with him as a passenger in the cab of the lorry.

Rolf was trying to pass a cyclist pedalling in the same direction. As he did so, a twig from a hedge came in through the open right-hand window of the cab. The twig caught the passenger in his right eye, which was so badly damaged that it had to be removed.

Rolf was tried in the magistrates' court for causing his passenger to be injured. I represented the passenger and declared that my brother was responsible for the injury through careless behaviour while overtaking the cyclist.

My speech found favour with the magistrates' court, which sentenced my brother to prison.

I had the remaining six siblings brought to me and spoke to them, "See what happened to Rolf!"

My siblings said, "You seem so sure that you're in the right. But what you don't know is that Rolf has gone to a higher court and appealed the sentence."

Rain. I was summoned to the court of appeal for further proceedings. The court of appeal confirmed the sentence handed down by the magistrates' court. Rolf went to prison.

I said to my siblings, "Now do you see what happened to Rolf?"

My siblings: "Why are you so anxious to punish us?"

Me: "The law should apply equally to all and it would not be right for me to make an exception for you."

The 10th of April. Rain. Ingvar's name-day. Ingvar was in prison. There was no pressing reason to mark his name-day with any kind of celebration.

My brothers Nils and Sven took the train north to Stockholm.

My siblings stood at Central Station as they departed and shouted, "Good luck, Nils and Sven!"

I talked to my remaining siblings, to my four sisters Gertrud, Sofia, Ragnhild and Gunhild, "People tend, with some justification, to distinguish between subjective individuals and objective individuals. For the former, things and events have meaning only to the degree that they impinge on their own selfhood. For objective individuals, things and events have meaning in themselves and their own selfhood merges with them. I belong without doubt to the objective individuals."

My siblings: "It sounds as if you're in a grave."

The 15th of May. Rain. Sofia's name-day was not celebrated.

Nils and Sven were taken on as cloakroom attendants

at the Strand Hotel in Stockholm. A lady left a musquash coat with them for safekeeping. On leaving the hotel my brothers gave her back a coat which she declared not to be the one she had handed in.

Nils and Sven were summoned to appear before the magistrates' court. I represented the lady. I made the case that the fur had gone missing because of negligence on the part of my brothers.

The magistrates' court sentenced them to prison. They tried to have the verdict set aside. The court of appeal upheld the magistrates' court's verdict. They were sent to prison.

I assembled my siblings: "See what happened to Nils and Sven?"

They replied, "You don't want us to live on our own. Maybe you think we ought to die instead?"

The 15th of July. Variable cloud. Scattered showers. Ragnhild's name-day was not celebrated.

I assembled my siblings: "Bills of lading should be made out for the transportation of corpses in accordance with the regulations for the transportation of express goods. Freight charges for corpses should be paid at the place of dispatch."

The 27th of August. Thunder. Rain. Rolf's name-day. Rolf was in prison. No congratulations.

The 8th of October. Rain. It was Nils's name-day. Nils was in prison. No good-luck wishes.

I assembled my siblings. I said to them, "For a declaration of death, when the person suspected of being dead has disappeared, it is necessary for at least twenty years to have elapsed since the person's disappearance. An exception is made, with observation of a time-lapse of five years, when the person suspected of having died disappeared in war, in a vessel that sank, their life was under threat or they were born at least ninety years ago."

Gertrud, Sofia, Ragnhild and Gunhild went to Central Station and bought tickets to Västerås.

In Västerås they became the owners of a ladies' dress-shop. A lady visited the shop with the intention of purchasing a bathing-cap. She slipped on a little mat on the parquet floor. She fell and hurt herself so badly that she later died.

My sisters were tried in the magistrates' court. I represented the woman's family. I declared that the mat should have been attached to a rubber underlay.

My sisters objected that nothing had prevented the woman from seeing and taking note of the mat, and also that, as far as could be judged, the accident was the result of the woman's haste.

I declared that in one of the circulars sent out by the insurance firm Fylgia loose mats were held up as an example of shopkeepers becoming liable for damages.

My sisters objected that the fire and accident insurance company Skandinavien, with which their shop was insured, displayed no such examples of shopkeepers' obligations.

The magistrates' court dismissed my sisters' case and sentenced them to prison.

My sisters sought a pardon.
The court of appeal found no reason to issue a pardon.

I said to my sisters, "See how things go for you when you try to break the law like this the whole time? You just end up under lock and key."

The 4th of November. Rain. It was Sverker's name-day. Sverker was in prison. His name-day was not celebrated.

My sisters applied for a judicial review. I was summoned to the Supreme Court and led the case against my sisters.
The Supreme Court impartially ratified the sentence of the Appeal Court. My sisters went to prison.

All my siblings were in prison. I thought, "Here I am and there they are."

December. Sofia, Sven, Gunhild, Ingvar, Ragnhild, Sverker, Rolf, Nils and Gertrud were in prison. I wrote to them, "See what happens when you do such things?"

January. February. March. April. May. June. My siblings were in prison. I stayed awake at night. I visited the cathedral. I went in to all its rooms. I liked the grey sandstone from the area around Höör.

July. I remembered Japanese lacquer and wondered where one could buy cellulose lacquer.

August. My siblings were in prison. I went to the cathedral and looked at the restored astronomical clock.

September. My siblings' sentences were completed. They came out of prison. I stood by the gate of the prison and greeted them when they came out. Out of the women's prison. Out of the men's prison. I said, "Have you now, finally, during this period of punishment, made up your minds not to leave me again?"

My siblings packed their cases. I said, "You're not thinking of going off again. You're not thinking of packing your cases ever again. Not Strängnäs. Not Köping. Not Stockholm. Not Västerås. Not anything of that kind again."

October. My siblings were within arm's reach and within sight. Many days went by.

November. I asked my siblings, "Will you stay with me your whole lives?"
    They replied, "What else can we do when we're never allowed to do anything by ourselves?"

December. Snowfall. Cold. Snow on the ground. I went into the cathedral. The nave's four transepts. The walls of the choir. The doorways of the aisle. The great stairway in the choir. Into the transept chapel. The arms of the transept. Down to the mighty crypt.
    Up again to the clock. Its fine mechanism. Into the mouth. To the taste-buds. The taste-pores. The

tongue's papillae. Further into the olfactory regions on the uppermost nasal muscle and the partition between the nostrils.

Into the olfactory cells and the gustatory nerves and further along their delicate connections to the brain.

January. Snow. Sun. I went to Market Square and bought sweets. I assembled my siblings and offered them the sweets. I asked them, "Do you think I am old?"

My siblings: "You are not that much older than us."

Me: "Do you think I am old and tired?"

My siblings: "Not that much more tired than we are."

Me: "I am not old. I am not tired. I am not ill."

February. Snow. Sun. I assembled my siblings and said to them: "I have decided to embark on a new course in life. Henceforth I aim to devote myself to working in the area of patents. I want you to be my assistants."

My siblings: "We don't know that much about patents."

Me: "Working in the area of patents with special emphasis on the law relating to trademarks. I want you to be my assistants."

Them: "We don't know that much about trademark law."

Me: "I shall give you instruction in the subject and you will gradually become informed and knowledgeable. My little assistants. My little, little assistants."

Snow. Sun.

I quoted to my siblings from the law protecting trademarks: "Whoever within this realm pursues manufacturing or handicrafts, agriculture, mining, trade or other forms of employment may, in addition to having the right to use his name or firm as a trademark, acquire exclusive rights to use a particular trademark in order to distinguish, in general trading, his products from those of others, by registering in accordance with the provisions of this law."

I asked them, "Do you understand what that means?"

They replied, "We think it means that it is against the law when someone uses another person's trademark."

Me: "Yes, it is a crime."

My siblings: "That you can be punished for?"

Me: "Yes, of course. It is in the nature of things that a punishment follows a crime."

I asked my siblings: "Do you actually know what a trademark is?"

My siblings: "A mark on a product? A product with a mark?"

I explained to them: "There are two sorts of trademark. On the one hand word-trademarks, which are a word, like for example Lion, Hart or Swan. On the other hand figurative trademarks, which are a picture, like for example a lion, a hart or a swan. Trademarks are often combinations of words and figures, like Swan along with a picture of a swan, Hart along with a picture of a hart or Lion along with a picture of a lion."

I looked to the future with confidence.

I quoted to my siblings from the law on protection of trademarks: "Registration is refused for figurative trademarks which are not characterised by having such a unique form as to be suited to distinguishing the products for which the trademark is designed, in normal trading, from the products of other manufacturers."

My siblings asked, "What happens if the patents office has refused to register a trademark?"

I replied, "Then the person who applied to register the trademark has to find another trademark."

My siblings summoned me. They said, "We feel that your work for the patents office is of interest. We have been stimulated by your efforts to instruct ourselves in that area."

Me: "I am glad, and I hope that you will continue to enjoy being my assistants for all the remaining days of your life."

Them: "We have decided that in future we will not devote ourselves to assisting you in patent issues. We intend instead, on our own authority, to start selling products of our own choice and we shall give them names which we ourselves decide. We possess powers of our own. We are thinking of becoming independent traders. We are leaving you. We are packing our cases. We hope you will manage to get by all right on your own."

I said to my siblings, "I don't want you to go."

My siblings: "We're going anyway."

Me: "Remember that it's me who decides whether or not the products you wish to sell can have the names you want to give them. I am the representative of the patents office and you have to do what I say."

My siblings: "We can still go wherever we want just as much as we want to."

Me: "But where are you going?"

My siblings: "We will settle wherever a business person is welcome."

My siblings packed their cases and then went to Central Station and travelled away to their new places.

My brother Ingvar wanted to start selling machines for showing moving images. He wanted to give the machines the name of Biograph. I refused to register this name as it is a general description of a product which cannot be used for a particular product.

My sister Gertrud wanted to sell wheat-flour with the name Diamond. I refused registration because the name, as a designation of a particular precious stone, had no connection with the nature of the product.

My brother Sven wanted to sell lawn-mowers with the name Bravo. I refused registration because products may not have names of the type Biggest, Fine and Efficient.

I didn't bother with my siblings' name-days.

My brother Nils wanted to sell sweets with the name England. I refused, because that name is reckoned a mark of origin and marks of origin may not be used as product names.

My brother Nils said that the sweets in no way came

from England and that England could therefore not be any mark of origin.

I replied that England is always to be reckoned a mark of origin and that in that respect the actual origin of the product is neither here nor there.

My sister Gunhild wanted to sell sewing-machines with the name Favourite. I refused registration, as registration of names such as Superb or Favourite is not permitted.

My sister Sofia wanted to sell cocoa with the name Sport. I refused registration as there is no connection between the nature of the product and that name.

My sister Ragnhild wanted to sell crispbread with the name Crownbread. I refused registration as this name could lead to confusion with bread baked by the royal bakeries.

My brother Rolf wanted to sell bicycles with the name Romp. I refused registration since the word, as a general slang term, lacks the distinctive quality that would allow it to be used as a trademark.

My brother Sverker wanted to sell arrack punch with the name Popular. I refused registration as registration of names such as First-Class and Best is not allowed.

My siblings said, "You don't want us to succeed as business people."

Me: "I have not prevented you in any way from being business people."

My siblings: "But we are never allowed to register our products."

I replied, "I am refusing to register the names of

your products because the law on trademarks does not permit registration of such names. You could for example sell writing-paper with the name Mandolin. But instead you want to sell radios with the name Radio and arrack punch with the name Popular. Why do you want to do that? You know perfectly well that it isn't allowed."

My siblings: "We really want to sell radios with the name Radio and arrack punsch with the name Popular. But we don't want to sell writing-paper with the name Mandolin."

The days went by.

My siblings made preparations to sell products under names they had previously applied for and for which I had refused registration. I gathered my siblings together and quoted to them, from the law relating to trademarks, the punishments in force for infringements of the law in question.

My siblings: "You don't want us to succeed by our own efforts. You just want to spoil things for us."

My siblings began selling products under names which I had refused to register. I reported them to the magistrates' court. They were sentenced to prison. They appealed to the Court of Appeal. The Court of Appeal approved the sentence of the magistrates' court. My siblings appealed further to the Supreme Court. The Supreme Court approved the sentence of the magistrates' court. My siblings were locked up in prison.

All of my siblings were in prison. Gunhild, Nils, Sverker, Rolf, Sofia, Ingvar, Ragnhild, Sven and Gertrud.

I visited them in prison. The women's prison. The men's prison. I said to them, "Not Cinema. Not Diamond. Not Bravo. Not England. Not Favourite. Not Sport. Not Crownbread. Not Fun. Not Popular."

I visited my siblings in prison and said to them, "Now look where you've ended up. This is what happens when you don't do as I tell you. You end up under lock and key."

I visited my siblings in prison. They were silent. They were playing cards. I had fruits and treats with me and cheered them up by telling them stories from our time at the Lion Pharmacy.

January. February. March. I held my head and felt how heavy a brain can be. Thirteen hundred grams.

April. May. June. July. I went in through the cranium. In through the frontal lobe. To the central groove. Into the Sylvian fossa. Into the cerebral cortex. Into the hypothalamus.

August. September. October. My siblings were still in prison. Into the visual cortex. The ganglions. The inner capsule. The cerebrum.

November. December. The hippocampus. Broca's area. The medulla oblongata. Into every gram.

January. My siblings came out of prison. I called them to me and welcomed them back.

Many days went by.

I thought my siblings were listless. I said to them, "You must pull yourselves together. You must cheer up."

I said to my siblings, "Don't look so fed-up. Chins up, all of you."

Many days went by. How many days had passed?

January. I remembered the bottles of cellulose lacquer – in my father's shop. The faintly yellowish lacquer with its slightly sour smell.

I asked my siblings,, "Do you remember when you were my helpers and assistants? Do you remember when you slept in the Lion Pharmacy?"

January. I stayed awake night after night. I wanted to buy cellulose lacquer. Time passed. I didn't want to sleep.

My siblings: "You must understand that we have our own helpers and assistants these days. We have our own apartments and jobs."

January. I asked my siblings to listen to an imaginary legal case, "I book into a hotel in another town. I introduce myself as a commercial traveller in fabrics. I place an advertisement in the local newspaper telling the ladies of the town that by application to the hotel they can have an opportunity to study a consignment of unusual Indian handwoven dress fabrics.

"Ten or so women turn up at the hotel and I choose one of them. When she comes to the hotel room, I pretend that I keep the delicate fabrics in my case, which is displayed on a table. I explain to her that it is an Indian custom that the customer first drinks a toast with the seller.

"The woman drinks the preparation of camphor and morphine which I have prepared. She slumps in a daze to the floor and falls asleep.

"After a while I leave the hotel-room. I leave the key on the inside of the door and then, from outside, I insert my *oustiti* in the keyhole. I squeeze the lower part of the key and turn it, so that it looks as if the door has been locked from the inside. I leave the hotel assuring the porter that I am on an errand to the bank.

My siblings waited silently. I asked them, "Why don't you say something?"

They replied, "We thought there would be more to come, or an explanation of some kind."

Then silence. After a while, "What is an *oustiti*?"

I replied, "*Oustitis* vary in shape, but the principle is always the same. A pair of narrow, steel jaws hollowed out in a half-circle with ribbing to stop them slipping are inserted through a keyhole, clamped round the key and turned. At its best, an *oustiti* resembles flat-nosed pliers. But the jaws are narrow and round and on the inside hollowed-out and ribbed."

My siblings sat silent. I asked them, "Did you hear what I said?"

My siblings replied, "We didn't know that you were interested in such things."

I asked my siblings, "Do you remember father's stories about the Möller Pharmacy?"

I said to my siblings, "We know you have to go off to all your meetings and duties."

I asked someone, "Are you a doctor?"

I wanted my siblings to sit round me and listen to an imaginary legal case. They said, "We sometimes think you have a stone in your head."

I thought about the dates of my siblings' name-days. I knew I had a good memory.

January. I asked my siblings. "You are all drivers now, aren't you? You all drive cars now?"
 My siblings: "Yes, each of us has our own car."
 Me: "Do you have a Mercedes-Benz and a Ford and a Volvo?"
 Them: "Yes, we have all of them and more."

I asked someone, "Are you a nurse?"

I could smell antimony, mordant, asphalt, yarrow, bone ash, silver citrate, and neat's-foot oil.

I asked my siblings, "How sick am I?"

I said to my siblings, "I haven't stopped keeping abreast of your name-days. Gertrud the 17th of March, Sven the 5th of December, Gunhild the 30th of January, Sofia the 15th of May. Rolf the 27th of August. Sverker the 4th of November. Ingvar the 10th of April. Ragnhild the 15th of July. Nils the 8th of October.

Have I forgotten anyone?"

I asked my siblings, "Will I get well?"

I reminded my siblings that I had had many colleagues in the law.
    My siblings: "Yes. They're probably dead now."

I could smell tin polish, starch, fish glue, molten glass and cinnamon.

My siblings: "You told us about a kind of key that can turn keys around. We are wondering whether you're going to go away? Where would you go?"

I thought, "Stone withstands time."

I asked those people who came and went with ink, containers and thermometers, "Are you auxiliaries?"

Hardly anything ever happened. Not much happened. Very little was happening.

Someone said, "It's time to sleep."
    But I don't want to sleep.

I asked my siblings:
    "Why are you so silent? Are you as silent as you once were?"

I wanted to get higher up. I thought of the ground floor as common and designed for treatment of the simpler cases, while on the floors higher up they treated the more complex and urgent cases.

I wanted to reach the top floor.

January. I said to my siblings, "I'm still alive and I still have my health. I'm not dead and buried yet."

They replied, "You're just an ageing snowman."

I asked my siblings, "Do you remember how father used to call Martin's Square Ox Square?"

I asked my siblings, "Who is the proprietor of the Lion Pharmacy these days?"

I asked my siblings to think of the following case, "I consult a doctor for my back pains and am given a prescription for a small, one-off dose of morphine. I put a thin coat of cellulose lacquer over the front page of the prescription. I go to the pharmacy and the morphine is dispensed. After it has been dispensed the assistant in the pharmacy stamps 'Cancelled' on the prescription with a rubber stamp. The prescription is returned to me. Once home, I carefully rinse off the mark of the rubber stamp. The surface of the prescription looks completely clean. That same day I visit another pharmacy and received another dose of morphine. Do you understand?"

My siblings: "You must rest soon."

Me: "The following day I succeed in getting three doses of morphine. I discover that I can also wash away the ink with which the doctor has indicated the dosage. I change the dose to ten times as much.

I go to a pharmacy on the edge of town and have the prescription accepted. Do you understand?"

My siblings: "We worry when you talk about your back pains. And what is this pharmacy on the edge of town?"

There were visiting-times.

My siblings asked, "Are you hungry?"

I could smell kaolin, beaver oil, Parisian green, ink powder, soap-bark, chlorophyll, heath moss, burnt chalk and horse-fat.

I asked my siblings, "Are you all still alive?"
My siblings: "All of us are alive and are in good health."

I asked my siblings, "Do you remember the kites?"

I asked my siblings, "Have all of you come here?"
My siblings replied, "We've brought the fruit and sweets you're so fond of."

My siblings asked, "Do you want to pee?"

I asked my siblings, "Do you remember when we studied extra Latin?"
My siblings replied, "It was only you who studied extra Latin."

I asked, "How long is this going to go on for?"

My siblings: "We're doing fine. We have jobs we like and families. We have children and grandchildren. They all say hello."

Someone said, "Sleep assures good health."
But I did not want to sleep.

I asked my siblings, "Have you driven your cars to Köping, Jokkmokk, Dorotea and Eksjö?"
My siblings replied, "Yes, we've been there many times."

January. I collapsed.

I said to my siblings, "You have wrinkles."

My siblings gathered round me and said, "Listen to us now. You're tired and not in the best of health. We think you need to rest. We're going away for a bit now. We'll soon be back."
I said, "You have to be quiet. And you have to stay here."

People came and asked me questions.
I asked them, "Why does no one tell me anything?"

My siblings said, "Perhaps you would like us to move you to the window? You can watch the children playing outside."

Someone said, "Time for breakfast."

I said to my siblings, "Either I stay here and die or I go away."
   My siblings: "Where would you go?"
   Me: "Well, you go away all the time."

I asked, "What's wrong with me?"

I said to my siblings:
   "You could sing something for me."

My siblings:
   "We wanted to be evil. We wanted to hit your arms and injure your face. We wanted to poke you with sharp objects in the ears and eyes. But we can't be bothered to."

I tried to answer the questions that were put to me.

I asked my siblings, "Are you no longer tied to me?"

People came and asked, "Do you have any siblings?"
   I replied, "I have four sisters and five brothers."
   They: "What are their names?"
   Me: "Their names are Sofia, Gunhild, Ragnhild, Gertrud, Ingvar, Sverker, Rolf, Sven and Nils."
   They: "Where do your siblings live?"
   Me: "My siblings are here. They'll be coming soon to call on me."

I remembered something from one of my mother's songs: "Then from subterranean rivers rose utter madness up."

I said to a nurse, "My siblings often visit me. I hardly get any peace for them."

Somebody said, "Time for lunch."

I asked, "Have my siblings been here?"

Someone asked, "How long have you been here?"
  I replied, "Since last month maybe."
  Them: "Where were you two months ago?"

Someone said, "Good morning. Sleep well?"
  I replied, "I haven't slept."

I remembered that my mother said, "The kite takes the chicks."

I asked, "How long will this go on for?"

Someone asked, "If two apples together cost two kronor, how much do three apples cost?"

I thought I had come as far in as it went. How could I come yet further in?

I thought, "How many minutes do I have left?"

I said, "Everyone is going. Why are they all going?"

I asked an auxiliary to listen carefully to the following sentences, "This traitor ought to be shot. May he be shot. Oh, if someone would shoot him."

Someone said, "Time to go to bed now."

I thought my siblings were nearby.

I remembered my mother talking about the planet Mercury. Or the planet Mars. Their long orbits.

I asked the doctor, "Has anyone contacted my siblings?"

I said to an auxiliary, "I'm leaving. How do I leave?"

I said to a nurse, "Let him be shot."

I thought I was looking for my siblings.

They asked, "Why are we asking you about all sorts of things?"
    I replied, "To find out if I know."
    They asked, "Why do we want to do that?"

Someone said, "Time for dinner."

I said, "A swarm of bees is attacking the person resting."

Everyone was whispering. I heard them whispering.

I thought, "How can something finish?"

I said to those people who were asking me questions, "Sleep and old age are poisonous."

I said to those people who were whispering, "I know you are whispering. You whisper all the time."

January. I thought I was searching around the Institute for the Feeble-Minded. Searching by the Blind Institute. Searching around the School for the Deaf and Dumb. Searching around the Isolation Hospital. Searching around the Ribbingska Nursing Home for the Incurably Ill.

I thought it was winter and that I could feel the cold spray of rain mixed with snow against my head. That I was walking along Klostergatan and I could feel that the soles of my shoes were wet and cold. That I was walking to Market Square and that I could see pine needles and bits of bark still lying on the ground after the sale of Christmas trees.

That I went to Central Station and looked. That they were not in the waiting-room. Not on the platforms. That a train was standing in the station and that I walked the length of the train looking into the carriages. The restaurant car. First class. Second class. The mail carriage. That I bought a ticket and took a seat by the window in an empty compartment. That the train departed and that the heater in the compartment was hot against my knees.

I thought I looked out through the window of the compartment at heaths and mosses with my forehead pressed against the window-pane, which felt cold. That it was snowing. That the train stopped in a town and then in a town smaller than the last one and then in an even smaller town which perhaps was not a town but a little village. That we travelled through forests. That the train, keeping its speed up, passed small stations. That I looked out through the window and looked to see if my siblings were out there.

That I noticed two skiers alongside the track whom I lost from sight when they turned off into the forest. That it snowed.

I thought that a head guard announced our arrival. That I got off and stood for a while on the platform. That the air was fresh and cold. That I stood still on the platform watching the snow fall. That I wondered if my siblings were thinking of me and talking to each other about where I was living and what I was up to. That I saw high mountains far away and other high mountains even further off, many white mountains, the mountains furthest away perhaps in Norway.

I thought I saw some rail workers uncoupling the locomotive from the carriages and coupling up another locomotive at the other end for the return journey. That I saw the head guard and the driver sitting on the footplate of the locomotive's cab. That they were smoking and that I could hear music from the cab, perhaps the driver's favourite music broadcast by a radio station. That he was tapping out the beat with one foot. That he and the head guard were talking to each other and looking around every so often. That their cigarettes burnt out and that they lit new ones.

I thought that they were killing time while they waited for the train's departure back to Central Station in Lund. That I walked a few paces away from them along the platform. That I then stopped and stood quite still. That I turned round towards them and saw them looking at me for a while.